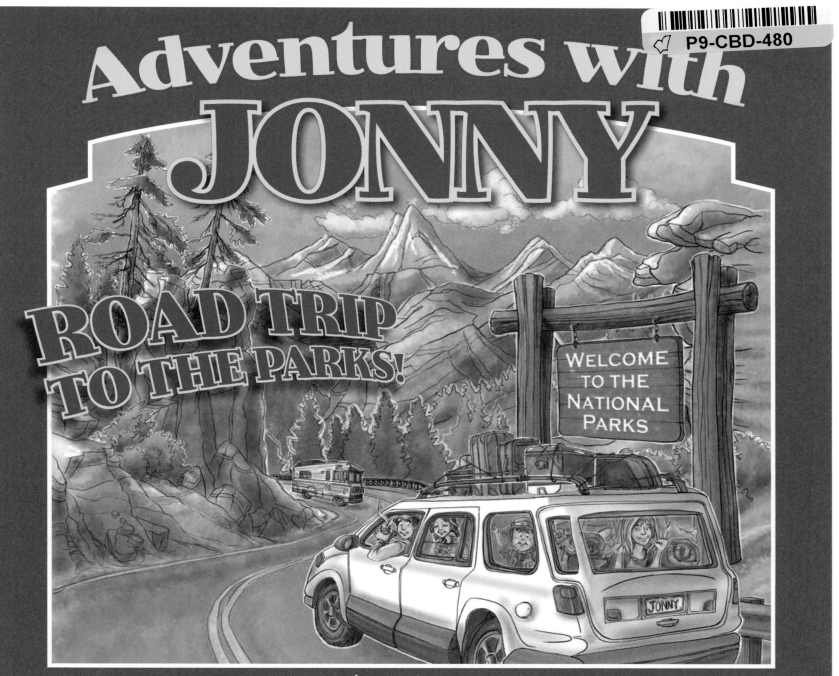

Adventures with JONNY

ROAD TRIP TO THE PARKS!

WELCOME TO THE NATIONAL PARKS

A family travel guide to the U.S. and Canadian national parks

Michael A. DiLorenzo

Illustrated By Jenniffer Julich

Running Moose Publications, Inc.
Clinton Township, Michigan

Printed in Canada

Published by
Running Moose Publications, Inc.

42400 Garfield Road

Clinton Township, MI 48038

Publisher's Cataloging-in-Publication Data
DiLorenzo, Michael A.

Adventures with Jonny : road trip to the parks / Michael A. DiLorenzo. – Clinton Twp, MI : Running Moose Publications, 2012.

p. ; cm.

Summary: A family travel guide to camping, hiking and enjoying the U.S. and Canadian National Parks.

ISBN13: 978-0-9777210-3-0

1. National parks and reserves--United States--Juvenile literature.
2. National parks and reserves--Canada--Juvenile literature. I. Title.

E43.5 .D55 2012
917.04539—dc22   2011935725

Cover and interior illustrations by Jenniffer Julich
Cover and Interior design by Eric Tufford

Printed in Canada by Friesens Corporation,
First Printing, March, 2012

16 15 14 13 12 • 5 4 3 2 1

DEDICATION

I have dedicated this book to Matthew Mannette, who for the too short of time that he was here, taught all who encountered him that we should do more than just go about life with minimal effort. In Matthew's eyes, LIFE was meant to be lived to the fullest, making the most of yourself and the most of the time that we are gifted to spend with our family and friends, being the best that we can be, at whatever the task to which we set our mind. Matthew knew that, for himself and for everyone else, our finish line is a virtual unknown and because of that, our time should never be squandered. Matthew taught us to not just live each day, but to THRIVE throughout each and every day that we awake.

This book is also dedicated to my mom and dad and to all the moms and dads that have packed their family in the car and hit the road to adventure. Despite endless miles, construction traffic or squabbling kids, they made their destination and more importantly, generated priceless, lifelong memories for all of us along the way. From all of us in the backseat, we thank you whole heartedly for the Road Trip Adventures.

ABOUT THIS BOOK

Adventures with Jonny, Road trip to the Parks, follows our unique Jonny book format, combining both entertainment and education to help bring more kids outdoors. However, recognizing that the most difficult aspect of a family road trip are the long hours of travel, the story portion of this book was created to extend a child's time spent within its pages. Each illustration, within the story portion of the book, is filled with numerous search items for your children to discover. There are different search items on each page, designed to help develop childrens sense of perception and increase their ability to identify hidden items. This skill will be tested on your Road trip Adventure as they search for resident animals in each Park that they visit. As with each book in the award-winning Adventures with Jonny series, our crafty illustrator leaves her mark with her telltale abbreviated name "JNNFFR" also hidden within each story illustration.

Please travel to the Visitor Center in the rear of this book or visit the Adventures with Jonny website to see where each item is hidden within the story pages of Jonny's Road trip to the Parks. While at our site, please let us know about your own family road trip adventure and the parks that you visited, with a brief story and picture for our Jonny's Road Trip Travel Album.

Let's Hit the Road!!

? TABLE OF CONTENTS

1

2

3

4

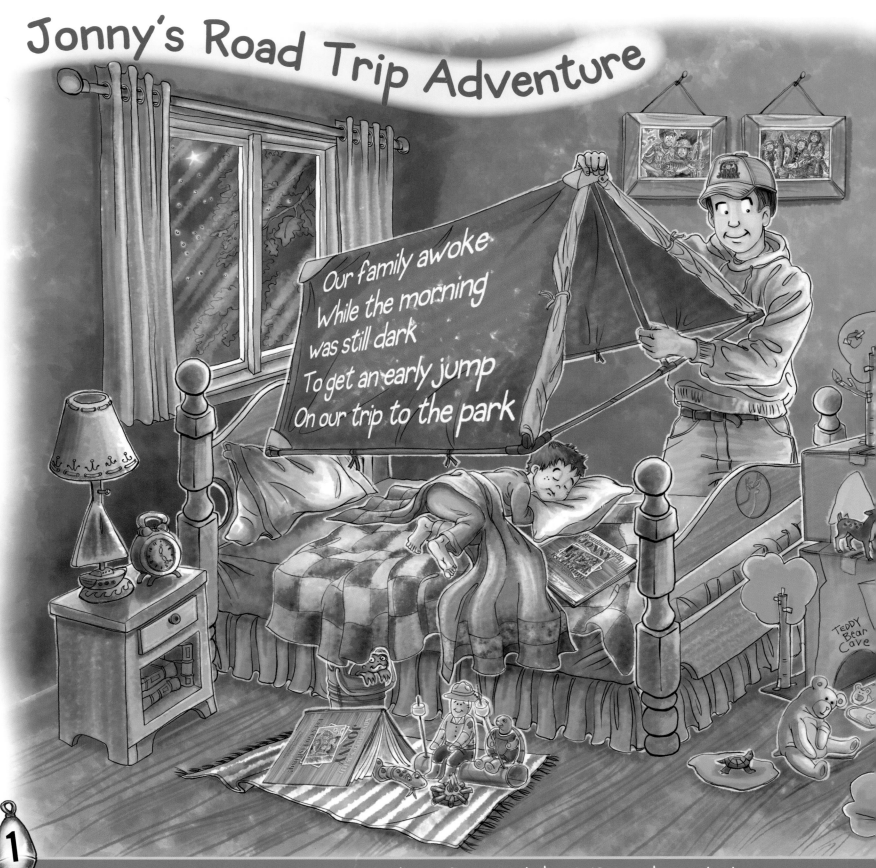

Jonny's Road Trip Adventure

Our family awoke
While the morning
was still dark
To get an early jump
On our trip to the park

TEDDY Bear Cave

1

FUNTIVITY #1

Jonny books are fun to read, there's 19 items here indeed,
Can you find them from our other books? Give the picture plenty of looks.

Our plans had been made
Our gear was in the car
We pulled away from home
Under the guidance of a star

1. Three Jonny books: Let's Go Fishing, Ice Fishing, Bows Does & Bucks 2. Two red buckets 3. Two frogs 4. Two turtles 5. Teddy Bear 6. Deer 7. Moose 8. Seagull 9. Tacklebox
10. Creel basket 11. Bobber 12. Rod/reel 13. Fishing net 14. Fishing hat 15. Two Jonny Logos 16. Fishing vest 17. Three framed fish 18. Two framed Jonny pictures 19. Two sinkers

FUNTIVITY #2 Although at home we left our pet, we brought along the alphabet.

When we awoke we were far from the city

The mountains were so **HUGE**
They made us all feel
itty-bitty

FUNTIVITY #3

We each have a name, that is not the same, and so does each park, to which we embark. Find these 10 National Parks:

1. Fundy 2. Pukaskwas 3. Glacier 4. Grand Canyon 5. Banff 6. Redwood 7. Yellowstone 8. Everglades 9. Acadia 10. Jasper

FUNTIVITY #4

A family meal has a lot of appeal and there are things while we eat, that make dining so neat. Can you find the following items...

1. Six cups 2. Two food baskets 3. Six stools 4. Eight people 5. Four ketchups 6. Four salt shakers 7. Four sugar jars 8. Four mustards 9. Four napkin holders 10. Six pies

FUNTIVITY #5   Roadside Diners are fun, not generic, the hidden items here you will find are numeric... Find the numbers 1 through 20.

9

We hit the visitor center
And chatted it up with the rangers

They told us of great trails
And how to avoid any
DANGERS

...Look for 20 arrow heads, amongst the words you have read.

Before our hike
And long before night
To the campground we went
To set up our site

FUNTIVITY #8

With a little luck, find all the gear we took from our truck:

1. Three backpacks 2. Cooler 3. Teddy Bear 4. Lantern 5. Flyswatter 6. Stove in case 7. Propane kit

8. Two sleeping bags 9. Four suitcases 10. Flashlight 11. Fishing gear 12. Red bucket

Then Dad said, "Let's take a hike"
He had ten miles in mind
So we shot him a look,
grabbed the trail book
And took a hike of a lesser kind

FUNTIVITY #9   Jonny logos on this page number 16, take a close look, so all can be seen!

12

The trailhead had begun
Winding through a twisty pine alley
That led us to a very high bluff
Overlooking a sun-filled valley

Elk and deer
were everywhere
Doing their
daytime grazing
This view was to our family
Nothing short of amazing

14

We continued on our hike
To a great waterfall
My teenage sister said,
"You won't see that
at any mall"

15

FUNTIVITY #11

Out on our hike, we brought our backpacks, can you find at this river all 8 animal tracks?

Mom whipped out her camera
And said, "Picture time, please"
Pushed us into a group
And then we all said

"CHEESE!"

We stopped for a break
By a babbling little creek
That's when we saw a snake
And my sister did the

FREAK

16

After our hike it was a rest that we did wish
But then Dad grabbed the rods and said, "Let's catch a fish!"

FUNTIVITY #12   The sun is so bright, it gets in our eyes...

We tied on some flies

And cast our lines about

Then the water
ERUPTED
as Kailey
hooked a trout

18

...so can you help me find our 28 flies?

We drove,

we hiked,

we fished

All in just one day

Was there much more that we could do Before we hit the hay?

19

FUNTIVITY #13

Out in the woods, you're never alone, in fact in this picture, there are 26 pine cones.

Well a sunset was to be
The next thing that we did see
The horizon blazed in orange
With my family next to me

The day
drew to a close
As we settled in our site
Where we built a warm bonfire
Under a starry, starry night

20

Fireflies are on their way, 84 you could say, find 7 sets of 7 flies
and 5 sets of only their glow that are seen by your eyes

Mom surprised us all
When she ran to the camp store,
And returned with the goods
For us all to make
S'MORES

Kell's was
cooked just right
My marshmallow caught

FUNTIVITY #15   Hopefully critters don't give you the jitters...

Kailey's too was perfect
Dad's was big
as a TIRE

22

We relived the day
And all that we did see

Nature offers us so much
That you can't see on T.V.

Crashing in our tents
For some much-needed sleep

FUNTIVITY #16   In the city, I am alive, but it is outdoors that I truly can THRIVE.

My name is Jonny, and this is my rockin' Road Trip adventure!

Today our family made memories

That forever we will keep

Kell's Journal Thrive

24

A VISIT TO THE PARKS

A visit, by definition, means to stay but for a short time. However, a family road trip adventure to a U.S. or Canadian national park is more like a reverse visit. It creates a memory that moves in and stays with you for life. The shared family experience of traveling to an unfamiliar destination, experiencing the magnitude of nature, and catching glimpses of elusive wildlife that are rarely seen otherwise are permanent souvenirs that last much longer than t-shirts of the trip.

The park lands of our own and neighboring countries feature magnificent natural creations that cannot truly be experienced through a screen or headphone. The only way to truly experience these lands is to travel deep inside their boundaries and absorb through all your senses what they have to offer. These rides through nature are the ultimate in amusement parks, and there aren't any height restrictions!

Though a national, provincial, or state park may be your destination, a large part of the adventure lies in the travel. Road trips let you taste what the rest of the country has to offer. There is so much more to each country than just the areas where we live, work, or go to school. There are unique personalities in the various regions, in the various residents, and in the histories that have shaped each and every little area of our countries. To travel through them is to harvest an education of our lands that goes well beyond the instruction available in a textbook.

The travels, the trips, and the tours are all part of an amazing adventure that awaits us when we depart the comforts of home and head down the highways and byways to our great national parks. Pick your park, pack your bags, load the car, and truly enjoy the ride!

⚠ WARNING! SAFETY TIPS

Park lands were created by Mother Nature, not a safety engineer. The wild presents many risks that are inherent to the territories in which you have travelled. However, simple and practical prevention can avoid injury or tragedy while on your travels. Common Sense is the most vital safety item that you can bring with you on your travels, and you can't pack too much of that!

Just a word of caution on the following items ...

a. **Poison ivy** - Leaves of 3 are not for me!

b. **Poison oak -** Is not a joke!

c. **Insect nests -** All are best left alone in their home.

d. **Cliff edges** - Always keep a safe distance.

e. **Waterfalls / Hiking** - The steady mist from a waterfall will keep surrounding rocks / trails wet and potentially very slippery. Be cautious when approaching falls on foot.

f. **Waterfalls / Swimming** - Dangerous currents can exist near the pool at the base of the falls. Avoid the immediate area directly beneath a powerful waterfall.

g. **Rapidly flowing rivers** - Can sweep you off your feet. River bottoms can be slick.

h. **Warning signs -** Heed all, they are there for the protection of both the visitor and the animals in the park or the grounds themselves that you drove so far to see.

i. **Wildlife** - Is just that, wild! It's in their name and their behavior can change in a heartbeat if they, or their young, feel threatened or become startled. Enjoy wild animals from a distance for your safety and theirs.

j. **Visual distance -** Throughout the entirety of your Park adventure, always stay within visual distance of each family member.

k. **Instincts -** Follow them. Just as the animals in the parks must do to survive, trust your instincts.

Poison Ivy

Poison Oak

HIKING TIPS

Once you are on your hike, you have only yourselves to rely upon for safety, and the items that you have packed out with you. Bring a light backpack with a first aid kit, including sunscreen and bug repellent.

a. Before you start your walk, check kids hiking boots / shoes to ensure they are tied and properly fit to avoid any tripping or blisters. Check your own boots too.

b. Hiking clothes aren't supposed to be trendy. They need to fit comfortably and allow the body to bend where it is supposed to.

c. When you approach a log in the trail, step over the log as damp logs can be very slippery.

d. If wildlife spotting is key, early morning hikes are more productive.

e. Avoid hiking in the heat of the day, if at all possible. High temps and strenuous physical activity can quickly shorten the entire family's supply of patience and interest level.

f. Maximum hiking distance and difficulty level is directly linked to children's abilities, not to the adults.

g. Discovery Hikes! Make some hikes goal oriented by coming up with a small list of things you could see in the area where you are hiking. You could include animals, plants or main points of interest. Look for your search items as a family unit and check items off your list as each is discovered.

h. Don't set out if weather is questionable or a storm is pending.

i. Don't set out if darkness is near.

j. Stay on the trail as it will always lead you back to safety.

k. If lost, stay put and blow the whistle periodically. The international distress signal is three hits.

l. Don't overload backpacks. Backpacks should carry just the essential items for your hike, including your trail map, compass or GPS, camera, binoculars, water, trail snacks, first aid kit, emergency blanket and a rain jacket.

m. Conservation is Key. Please leave the park and the trail system better than you found it. All garbage comes out with you and if you come across some that was left behind by a careless, mindless hiker, bring theirs out with you too.

n. If your goal is to see wildlife while on your hike, pack along your inside voices and use them while on your trek. Be considerate of other hikers who may be on their search for wildlife and keep the voices down when in their company. If wildlife has been spotted by your family or others, keep the noise to a minimum so that all can enjoy the exciting wilderness experience.

o. If your hike will be taking you through bear habit or that of other dangerous game (like sleepy teenagers), outside voices are highly recommended along the way so the animal hears you long before you ever see them and will not be spooked by your sudden appearance on the trail. Startled animals can be very dangerous. Also, if you are going to be in bear territory, pack along a can of pepper spray just in case.

p. Never start a hike without a compass and a bearing in which you will be traveling and by which you will be returning. Along the way, take notes of landmarks and where they are located in relation to the trail.

q. Leave a hiking trip itinerary with a friend or family member back home and leave a copy under your driver's car seat as well.

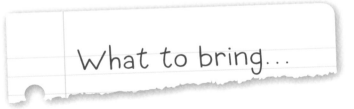

What to bring...

Whistle

Perhaps one of the greatest joys of traveling with your family to a U.S. or Canadian national park is the peaceful departure from civilization that takes place as you near your destination. However, along with this separation, comes a vast distance between you and any stores that hold the necessities of your family's trip. Make sure that all the necessities are packed before you go. Here are some of the key items that you will need to make your Road Trip to the Parks a great experience for the whole family:

So here, in an outlined nutshell, are things you will want to have with you:

a. **Backpack** (essentials only, keep it light)

b. **Water bottle** (drink before you're thirsty)

c. **Hiking boots** (you buy em', you break em', and then take them hiking)

d. **Compass / GPS** (always brings you home)

GPS

e. **Weather radio** (know before you go)

f. **Binoculars** (brings the far out, close in)

g. **Camera** (capture the memories)

h. **Sunscreen / bug juice / after bite / first aid kit** (because Stuff Happens!)

i. **Rain jacket** (because Weather Happens!)

j. **Trail maps** (know where to go)

Trail Map

k. **Sunglasses** (provides geek-level protection, while looking cool)

l. **Hat** (cap the chimney)

m. **Flashlight / head lamp / clip on light** (park nights can be oh so very dark)

n. **Emergency blanket** (again, Stuff Happens!)

o. **Bright colored t shirt or hat** for each family member (can't find what you can't see)

p. **Whistle safety** (3 blasts for help, for that matter, 3 of anything means help)

Compass

q. **Flip flops or sandals** for trips to park bathrooms and showers (clean feet are happy feet)

CAMPING TIPS

Pre trip preparation is likely the best way to ensure a grand time with your family while on your camping adventure. Use a list to pack your items, double checking to make sure the necessary items have been accounted for. Be familiar with ALL of your gear and how to set it up before you ever leave your house. A pre-trip family practice campout in your backyard prior to your trip, will give you a feel for the key things that you will need and how to use them. This is a fun and very functional way to prepare for your trip.

a. Site selection. Just like buying a house, your camp site is real estate on a small scale so think location, location, location. Consider the view, the traffic within the campground and the proximity of your site to the bathrooms/bathhouse if young bladders are in camp. Also, consider your site's closeness to the pool or playground to keep an eye on older children or to minimize your constant treks with younger kids.

b. Site prep. This is most important for tent set up. Choose the most level part of your site and clear it of any sticks or stones as they will hurt your bones (when you sleep on them through the night). Bringing along a small landscape rake can quickly give you a very clean, stick-free tent site. A small whisk broom will keep a clean tent floor inside too.

c. Think rain. Avoid setting up your tent in a low spot or depression within your site. Rain is always a possibility and waking up in a pond is just not fun, unless of course, you're a duck!

d. Daylight set up. When possible, get your campsite set up during daylight hours as it makes the whole process so much easier and you don't lose stuff you know you darn-well packed!

e. Keep flashlights readily accessible prior to turning in for the night.

f. Check the weather before you turn in and if rain is in the forecast, prep your site by dry-storing all items that you do not want to get wet. Bring rain gear into the tent so that you don't get soaked looking for it outside in the morning. Remember, dew will do a light rain's job by coating everything during the night, so again, dry-pack accordingly. Dry campers are truly happier campers!

g. Check your tent and all items before you leave and make repairs or fix leaks before departure.

h. Bring a rain tarp for over the tent and a ground tarp for under the tent. Be sure the ground tarp does not extend past the tent base so that it does not collect and then channel water underneath your tent.

i. Store food properly and securely. Remember, animals find food primarily through their sense of smell and people food smells travel a long way. Secure food in a cooler and place it in your vehicle or elevate it if necessary. This goes the same for any food scraps that may be in your garbage.

j. Reservations. Make reservations long in advance if you want a particular site or if you want to reserve a site that you stayed at previously. Additionally, if you will be spending any nights in a park lodge or dining in a park restaurant, reservations are needed well in advance for peak season visits. A year out is not too long in advance.

Pre-Trip Tips and Key Items

a. Set up your entire camp in your backyard and have a practice camp out, relying on nothing from your house. This includes having your meals outdoors. This will truly show what you need and what you do not. Yes, I said this again as it's that important to make sure you have everything and know how to use it before you go.

b. Load fresh batteries in all, flashlights, GPS, cameras, electronic devices.

c. Pack vehicle charging cords for other electronic devices.

d. Fill lanterns with kerosene and check each mantle. Bring extra mantles.

e. Fill stoves or grill with fuel. Pack additional fuel based on length of your stay.

Lantern

f. Pack foul weather gear, which is primarily a waterproof shell, for each family member. Select gear that is big enough to fit several layers of clothes underneath it. This will extend it's seasonal use for adults and add a number of seasons in which it will fit a growing child.

g. Break in the boots before you go and bring moleskin or bandaids for the blisters that will decide to join you on your hike.

h. If taking a camper or motor home, run through a complete maintenance checklist well in advance of your trip and tend to each item in need before takeoff. Also, create an inventory list and stock your home away from home with all necessary items, making sure to work off the list so that key items are not forgotten prior to departure.

i. Consider your vehicle to be part of your family and make sure it's healthy before you go, taking care of any necessary maintenance before you pile on the miles.

j. Proper tire inflation alone can increase your mileage and over a long trip, this can add up to big savings. Make sure your spare tires for your car, truck, camper or travel trailer are all in good condition and that you have the necessary tools to change a tire, readily accessible should the need arise.

k. If you have a pet, make arrangements well in advance for its care while you are on your trip. If your pet is going with you, verify the acceptance of pets in the parks you are visiting before you hit the road. Bring your pet's necessary care items as well, and keep the leash at the ready so you don't have to dig for it during travel pit stops.

l. Pack well in advance of your trip and work off of a list so that you don't forget vital items that will be costly to replace on your travels. Your trip is not a surprise to you, so don't pack at the last minute as if it just suddenly came up.

m. Chat with other folks you know, who have similar interests and lifestyles to your families or who have made the trip to the parks before, to key you in on what to see and what not to see.

n. Use the Internet to gather all the information you can on your destination park before you go and print off key travel maps or hiking trails and keep these with your travel log.

TRAVEL TIPS

US 66

Regardless of where you decide to camp or hike, you have to get there and get back home. Since travel can comprise a significant part of the trip, it should be scheduled to be as fun and entertaining as possible, as it is all part of the experience.

a. DON'T OVER PACK! Your vehicle will be squished, and it will be difficult to find everyone's stuff along the way. Organize items as you pack, keeping like items together.

b. Pack items in order that you will need them. Most likely you will have to set up camp before you go fishing, or whatever your destination activities may be. Pack the fun stuff in your vehicle first and then the camping items so that you can readily access camping gear first when you arrive at your destination park.

c. Think Memories and take pictures at the key areas that can jog your memories years down the road, including park entrance signs, states welcome signs, and iconic park landmarks. Capture the unspectacular as well along the way to remember the subtleties of your family's road trip adventure. Sleeping shots in the car of gaping-mouthed family members are always a comedic reminder of your travels.

d. Think Memories and the lack thereof as you age, so keep a log and write things down as they happen or as you visit them. Make note of a great diner or outfitter that you would return to or recommend to someone who might be traveling in that area in the future.

e. Don't overload the schedule and try to do too much.
Don't pack pressure on your trip!

f. Leave the work at home. Do not get caught up in checking emails, voicemails and work texts, having this constantly interrupt time with your family. Sound planning for your work departure is key to keeping it at bay while you are away.

g. If on a multi-day road trip, pack an overnight bag with the entire family's nightly and morning needs, and pack this bag last. Then, when you pull in for the night, only one bag needs to be unloaded for the entire family.

h. If stopping near a large city, while on a multi-day travel, try to stay on the destination side of the city so that your morning departure does not begin in a lengthy, time-delaying, patience-eating, and largely aggravating traffic jam that is inbound to the city.

i. Pack a healthy supply of snacks and drinks from home to save on the high cost of convenience store or fuel station items and their lack of healthy alternatives. A gallon of water in a cooler and each person's water bottle is the most cost-effective way to go.

j. Avoid dairy products for drinks when you can, as an in-transit drink. One milk spill in the back seat can leave your ride a tad stinky long after your trip is over.

k. When possible, travel secondary highways to get a flavor of the area you are traveling through which is often times missed by interstate highway travel.

l. Eat at Local Diners along the way or at your destination to get a taste of the foods in the area and to visit with the locals who have intimate knowledge of the area and can direct you to hot spots not written about in any travel guides. Engage their staff in conversation about the things to see and do in the area, that they can recommend and more accurately depict, than a colorful marketing brochure.

m. If traveling through large cities, try to schedule inner city travel time around rush hour peaks.

n. Bring road music! Make sure these are tunes that appeal to the whole family so that you truly enjoy them as you travel down the road. These tunes will stay with your child as a lifetime reminder of your trip. Hearing John Denver's "Country Roads" still packs me in the backseat of the family car, jammed in with my siblings, bound for vacation, long years after those trips have gone by.

ROAD GAMES

The toughest part of a road trip is keeping everyone entertained while traveling to your park destination. A tougher struggle now exists when you try to pry children's eyes off of electronic devices and focus their attention outside on the many great things you have driven to see. Bring on the family road games, where the game board is all things outside. Every family has their favorite road game to play and many are twists or twisted variations of the same game played over the years by traveling families. Here are some family favorites that will help pass the miles with a fun flair to each.

a. **Alphabet Game**

   i.   The goal of the Aphabet Game is to find, in order, words that start with each letter of the alphabet. The words must be found outside the vehicle in which you are traveling. The words can be on other cars, trucks, billboards, road signs or buildings. The game can be played with a single point applied to each word that someone finds with the winner being the person who has found the most words beginning with the correct alphabet letter. However, the game is commonly played as a family team game, with no score kept at all.

   ii.   The Alphabet Game can be played with a couple of twists to make it more interesting. Try playing the game working backwards through the alphabet or starting at a random letter within the middle of the alphabet. Be easy on your family, by allowing words with the letters Q, X, Y or Z found anywhere within the word to count for that letter.

b. **Billboard BINGO**

   i.   Billboard BINGO is similar to the alphabet game, but loosely based on the BINGO format. The goal of the game is for family members to identify words that start with each letter in the word BINGO. The search area for words must be outside of the vehicle and could be restricted to billboards only. Once one family member sees the word, it cannot be used by other family members. The first one to complete the spelling of the word BINGO is declared the winner. Just so everyone in the vehicle knows who completed their word first, upon completion of the word, the family member must yell the name of the word as loud as they can!

c. **Billboard BINGO National Parks Style**

   i.   Billboard BINGO can be played with a park-based theme by using national, state, or provincial park names in place of the word "bingo." Therefore, your family could be playing "Billboard Yosemite" or "Billboard Banff." Once again, whoever completes the word first is declared the winner, but not until they loudly yell out the completed park name.

d. **License Plate Game**

   i.   The goal of the License Plate Game is for the family to see how many license plates can be found from different states. It is most interesting to see how far folks will travel to get to their park destination. The License Plate Game can be played on several levels to keep it fun and interesting.

   ii. The game can be played over the entirety of the trip, from the time you leave home to the time you return. The game can also be played within individual states or provinces to teach which states/provinces have the most out-of-area visitors or within individual parks to see which parks draw the most out-of-area visitors.

e. **Road Kill Round-Up**

   i.   Gross? Maybe. Tasteless? Maybe. Fun and Educational? Absolutely. The Road Kill Round-Up Game is a competitive family game that teaches kids animal identification at a quick glance. Road Kill Round-Up also teaches awareness that animals can present a very serious road hazard as well as the most common areas where animals attempt road crossings. This information will subtly stay with children as they approach driving age and are responsible for their own safety and the safety of those traveling with them. The game also holds everyone's attention outside the vehicle, focused on the area that your family is traveling through.

   ii. Road Kill Round-Up is a points-based family game. Family members earn points in two ways, by being the first to spot a road kill and then by correctly identifying the poor critter. However, there are also two forms of penalties in which family members can lose points. First, points can be lost for a false call, which means improperly calling out a road kill that turns out to be anything but a dead critter. Second, points can be lost for misidentifying the species of the road kill. This point loss is referred to as an "ID blunder" or "blundered ID."

   iii. The Road Kill Round-Up winner is the first family member to reach fifteen points. Just as in other sports, there must be at least a two-point spread for the family member to be declared the winner. This simple rule alone can force stiff competition to the *finished* line.

   iv. Point system for Road Kill Round-Up:

        1. Two points earned for first person to spot a road kill

        2. Three points earned for first person to correctly identify that particular road kill

        3. Two points lost for a false call, misidentifying anything else as a road kill

        4. Three points lost for committing a blundered ID, incorrectly identifying the species of the road kill

        5. A scoring change can be applied to species identification by establishing your own point value for different animal species. Use a lower point score for common animals, assigning a point value of one to a possum and a higher point score to rare animals, such as a point value of one million to, say, a saber tooth tiger.

U.S. NATIONAL PARKS/ NATIONAL PARKS SERVICE

The national park system throughout the United State is nothing short of astounding, with well over three hundred combined national parks and national landmarks for your family to visit. The national parks include the most tremendous landscapes and waterscapes you could ever fathom, as well as historical landmarks that played a key role in the development of this awesome country. Truly, from sea to shining sea and from the southern border to our great Canadian neighbors, there are national parks in all corners of the country and widely spread throughout the bosom of the central states.

There is a vast difference in landscapes from park to park, offering visiting families a wide range of activities. Simply due to the ruggedness of the terrains of some parks, some are more appealing to families with younger kids and others are more appealing to families with older children.

Deciding which national park to travel to is best done with input from all family members. A child's reaction and interest levels can provide an eye-opening perspective. Some regions of the country will have multiple national parks located in close proximity to one another, allowing you to visit several parks while on your road trip adventure. Do not overlook the national parks you may be driving by on the way to your destination park, since visiting additional parks on the way can give your family the opportunity for a real parks extravaganza of a trip.

Prior to your trip, do as much research as possible on the parks you are traveling to so that your family can see as many of the great landmarks as possible for which any given park is well known. The National Park Service website at nps.gov is a great place to start the planning of any road trip to the U.S. national parks.

Junior Ranger Program

The Junior Ranger Program is an interactive program designed to engage kids in educational activities at many of the national parks. Each park has its own program and a nominal fee for children to participate. To be a junior ranger, stop at the visitor center of any participating park, pick up your booklet, and take part in the activities illustrated within the book. Oftentimes, this includes being involved in a ranger-led educational program. Upon completing the activities, stop back at the visitor center, show a park ranger your completed book, and receive your junior ranger patch. Some parks have junior ranger programs and patches for different age groups or seasons.

The National Park Service website at nps.gov also has an interactive, on-line junior ranger program that allows children to pretend to be a park ranger; it even lets them decorate their own ranger office as part of the fun. The on-line ranger program can be a great way to get your children interested in visiting the parks as the trip approaches or to relive the experiences you had as a family upon returning from your road trip adventure!

National Park Service Passes

The America the Beautiful – National Parks and Federal Recreation Land Pass is required for entrance into any of the national parks and use of fee-charging federal recreation sites. The annual pass fee for most folks is eighty dollars at the writing of this book. However, for senior citizen residents of the United States age sixty-two or over, a lifetime pass costs only ten dollars. The senior citizen pass also provides a fifty percent discount on some expanded park programs. There is also a free pass available for disabled United States citizens with permanent disabilities, also inclusive of fifty percent discounts for some expanded park services. Finally, volunteers within the parks who acquire five hundred cumulative hours receive a free pass too. And, by the way, thank you for your service to the parks!

National Park Service Passport

The Passport to Your National Parks Program is a fun way to catalog your park adventures and record your trips to the various participating parks. The passport program began in 1986 through Eastern National, a National Park Service partner. The passport book is a 104-page, very condensed guidebook that includes national park maps and valuable visitor information. The book can be used to collect cancellation stamps and commemorative stamps as well as to record the location and date of your visit at various park locations throughout the country. This passport program provides the flair of international travel without having to leave the comfort and inner beauty of the United States!

Following is a random sampling of what some of the national parks have to offer your family, illustrating the vast differences in landscape, wildlife, and locations throughout the United States. In order to aid your understanding of the size of each park, please keep in mind that 640 acres comprises but one square mile.

The information within this section was obtained through personal travel experience, ranger interviews, and the national park website at www.nps.gov.

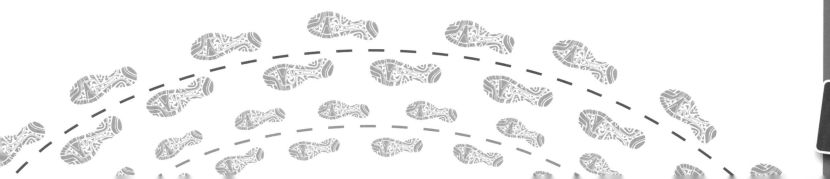

ACADIA NATIONAL PARK, in the southeast corner of Maine

Founded: 1919

How Big: At just over 47,000 acres, this is one of the smaller national parks, encompassing two islands and miles of very rugged, rocky Northern Atlantic Ocean shoreline.

Who Lives There: Some of the more unique species of wildlife that call Acadia home are harbor seals, moose, whales, peregrine falcons, and bald eagles, while more common animal residents include white-tailed deer, coyotes, foxes, and bobcats. There are also many excellent beaver viewing spots around the ponds within the park.

What's to Do: Hiking and birding are the most prominent activities within Acadia, with over 125 miles of hiking trails and numerous hot spots to view coastal waterfowl.

Cool Stuff: Twenty-six mountains are located within the park. Cadillac Mountain is the highest at 1,530 feet and is said to be the first place in the United States to get sunlight in the morning.

Thunder Hole is a rock formation along the Acadian coast that makes a thunderous sound when waves crash in (no lightning, but still very cool).

Jordan Pond Nature Trail is a 3.3 mile loop trail around the pond featuring wood plank trail sections, bridges, a rocky shore, and easy walking.

During low tide, a very temporary pathway is exposed, leading from the mainland to Bar Island. However, don't stay too long on the island and be wary of the quickly rising tide that can cover your return route to the mainland.

A historic carriage road system that crosses seventeen unique stone bridges offers a unique family travel experience and is a great biking trail.

The Night Sky Festival in September is a ranger-led program with great views of the Milky Way Galaxy and many constellations.

Junior Ranger Program: Yes...and Acadia National Park also has a Senior Ranger Program.

Park Neighbors: Lamoine State Park, Birch Point State Park, Eagle Lake, and Donnell Pond Public Reserved Lands

EVERGLADES NATIONAL PARK, in southern Florida

Founded: 1947

How Big: This park is a whopping 1.4 million acres! Much of the Everglades is water-infused, incorporating thousands of tiny islands within its boundaries.

Who Lives There: A very wild variety of animals call the Everglades home, including alligators, Florida panthers, dolphins, pilot whales, armadillos, and geckos, as well as several species of lizards, snakes, and frogs. The Everglades are also home to a vast array of birds, including heron, egrets, pelicans, and others.

What's to Do:	The Anhinga Trail is a short .8 mile trail that offers spectacular wildlife viewing, especially for birds and alligators. December to February are peak periods for wildlife activity along the trail.
	The Shark Valley Tram Tour is a two-hour narrated tour of the park providing fantastic science education and nature viewing.
	There is great fishing inside the park, and you are allowed to hire an outside guide to fish within the park, though you will need a Florida fishing license.
Cool Stuff:	This one-of-a-kind ecosystem is not duplicated anywhere on earth.
You Need to Know:	Do not try to get too close to alligators and absolutely do not attempt to feed the alligators, as there is not much difference to them between the food you have for them and the food you are to them.
	Bring your own food and drink to the park, as there are minimal places to acquire food within the park boundaries.
Junior Ranger Program: Yes	
Park Neighbors:	Dry Tortugas National Park, Biscayne National Park, Big Cypress National Preserve

GREAT SMOKY MOUNTAINS NATIONAL PARK, in Tennessee and North Carolina

Founded:	1934
How Big:	The Great Smokies are over 521,000 acres, with a landscape featuring sixteen mountains in excess of six thousand feet, the highest being Clingman's Dome at 6,643 feet.
Who Lives There:	Black bears, lots of them, since the Smokies provide the largest protected black bear habitat in the East. Approximate black bear population is 1,500 or roughly two per square mile. Other animals include white-tailed deer, coyotes, and bobcats. Interestingly, the NPS has reintroduced elk, river otters, and peregrine falcons to the park. There are over two hundred species of birds within the park and over fifty native fish, including brook trout, that call the park's enormous river system home. The Smokies are commonly referred to as "The Salamander Capital" with thirty-one species living in the park boundaries.
What's to Do:	Hiking is huge with over 850 miles of trails. History buffs love the park's nearly eighty historic structures, largely comprised of charming log buildings. The driving tour through Cades Cove features a log home village and active grist mill, which grinds corn into corn meal and makes great corn bread.
Cool Stuff:	The park's brook trout restoration program has been successful in producing excellent brook trout fishing throughout 2,115 miles of streams. Check to see if any stream sections are closed prior to casting your line. Finally, depending on which state you are in, within the boundaries of the park, you will need either a Tennessee or North Carolina fishing license.
Junior Ranger Program: Yes	
Park Neighbors:	Mammoth Cave National Park and Congaree National Park

BADLANDS NATIONAL PARK, in the southeast corner of South Dakota

Founded: 1978

How Big: This park comprises 244,000 acres of the most unbelievable, moonscape-like grounds, including pinnacles, buttes, and spires, as well as one of the largest mixed-grass prairie ecosystems in the entire country.

Who Lives There: Bison, bighorn sheep, pronghorn, and prairie dogs call the Badlands home.

The Badlands are also the site of the reintroduction of the black-footed ferret, the most endangered land mammal in North America.

What's to Do: Be awed by an amazing landscape and climb what look like giant anthills.

Attend the Night Sky Program, which wows visitors with amazing celestial views of over 7,500 stars and the Milky Way Galaxy as well as other star clusters and satellites.

Immerse yourself in lots of American Indian history and one of the world's richest fossil beds.

Cool Stuff: The Stronghold District of the park was used by the U.S. military as a gunnery range during World War II. The area was used for air-to-air and air-to-ground gunnery practice. Even today, areas of the ground within this district are littered with spent shell casings.

Junior Ranger Program: Yes

Park Neighbors: Wind Cave National Park, Mt. Rushmore National Memorial, and Devil's Tower National Monument, located in northeastern Wyoming

GUADALUPE MOUNTAINS NATIONAL PARK, on the western edge of Texas

Founded: 1966

How Big: This lesser known but exceptional park is 86,416 acres big.

Who Lives There: Mountain lions, fox, coyote, bobcat, badger, mule deer, javelin, snakes, and lizards call Guadalupe Mountains National Park home.

What's to Do: Hike Smith Spring Trail, a 2.3 mile loop that ends with a spectacular view. On your return trip, take time to look for fossils in rocks that were formed by a reef millions of years ago.

Hike to Manzanita Spring, which looks like a pond. This is a great place to see the birds and wildlife that are attracted to this rare resource in the desert.

Visit Smith Springs, which flows as a babbling brook and is surrounded by ferns, maples, and mandrone trees.

Cool Stuff: Sensational fall colors in McKittrick Canyon contrast with the arid Chihuahuan desert landscape.

This park is also home to another El Capitan, an ancient limestone reef that is the eighth highest peak in Texas.

Guadalupe Peak is the highest summit in Texas, standing 8,749 feet high.

Junior Ranger Program: Yes

Park Neighbors: Carlsbad Caverns just across the New Mexico border to the north and Big Bend National Park to the south along the United States/Mexico border

ISLE ROYALE NATIONAL PARK,

in Michigan's Upper Peninsula, smack dab in the middle of Lake Superior

Founded: 1940

How Big: Isle Royale is over forty-five miles in length and nine miles at its widest point, encompassing roughly four hundred tiny islands that dot its rocky shoreline.

Who Lives There: Moose and wolves are the two prominent island residents, with moose being the more visual of the two. Red fox are regular visitors at campsites. Bald eagles and the common loon are routinely sighted by guests on Isle Royale. Mink, muskrats, and beavers also reside on the island.

What's to Do: Hiking, backpacking, kayaking, canoeing, camping, and fishing are key activities within the Isle Royale boundaries. There are approximately 165 miles of hiking trails. Canoeists and kayakers can explore the coastline, but need to anticipate and properly train for lengthy, rough portages if going through the island's interior. The trails are infused with rocks and root systems in many areas, requiring hikers to keep more of an eye on their footing than on the awesome scenery surrounding them.

Fishing for northern pike is excellent on the inland lakes, but you will need to pack a collapsible rod for ease in transporting down the trail.

Kids enjoy the Daisy Farm beach, boardwalks over the beaver streams, and exploring the countless miles of rocky shoreline.

Cool Stuff: Leave the car keys behind. The only way to get to the island is by boat or seaplane. There are no motorized or wheeled vehicles on the island. Getting there is part of the adventure, with a somewhat lengthy boat ride as the final part of your trip. The boat tour from Houghton, MI, to Rock Harbor is approximately six and a half hours. The trip from Copper Harbor, MI, to Rock Harbor is just over three hours. The trip from Grand Portage, MN, to Windigo is approximately three hours. These are one-way time estimates that can vary based on water conditions. The boat rides take you across the surface of the largest freshwater lake in the world, Lake Superior, offering spectacular views of deep blue hues not seen on other waters.

Numerous shipwrecks dot the island coastline and some can be viewed from the Voyageur II ferry route.

Commercial fishing and copper mining were significant industries on the island during the late 1800s and early 1900s. Several historic sights are remnants of these days gone by. The Edison Fishery location provides a clear look at what the commercial fishing industry was like in its heyday.

Junior Ranger Program: Yes

Park Neighbors: Pictured Rocks National Lakeshore and Porcupine State Park, both located in Michigan's Upper Peninsula, and Apostle Islands National Lakeshore, on Wisconsin's north shoreline

YELLOWSTONE NATIONAL PARK,

in the northwest corner of Wyoming, in the southwest corner of Montana, and in the northeast corner of Idaho

Founded: 1872

How Big: So big it's in three states! This park is 2,219,789 acres big, of which ninety-six percent is in Wyoming, three percent is in Montana, and one percent is in Idaho. That's really big! This park has several mountains as permanent residences, the highest being Eagle Peak at 11,358 feet.

Who Lives There: A shorter list would include who doesn't. But some of the animals you might see on your trip include bison, grizzly bear, black bear, cougar, bobcat, wolf, lynx, elk, moose, bighorn sheep, mountain goat, pronghorn, mule deer, and white-tailed deer. Animals on the smaller scale include the badger, fisher, beaver, otter, weasel, coyote, fox, and the less-than-friendly wolverine. Bald eagles and ospreys are park regulars as well.

What's to Do: Tons! There are so many things to see in Yellowstone that it would take numerous days to see it all. A highlight is the Old Faithful Geyser, but this is just one of three hundred geysers within the park.

Mammoth Hot Springs and "The Grand Canyon of Yellowstone" are also outstanding sights.

Perhaps one of the most underrated but outstanding views is that of Lower Yellowstone Falls at Artist Point. Simply riveting!

Endless hiking and over 2,400 miles of blue ribbon trout streams offer some of the finest fly-fishing the world has to offer.

Cool Stuff: Yellowstone is America's very first national park.

The enormity of the park itself is humbling, and it contains perhaps the greatest variety of landscapes within one single park.

Old Faithful Lodge is one of the largest log structures in America.

People have more run-ins with bison than bears, so be cautious of the big fellas.

Yellowstone sits on one of the largest and most active volcano beds on earth.

On average, twenty-two forest fires a year are started by lightning strikes within the park.

Junior Ranger Program: Yes

Park Neighbors: Grand Teton National Park located just south of Yellowstone, Glacier National Park in the northwest corner of Montana, along the Canadian border, and Sawtooth National Recreation Area in central Idaho

GLACIER NATIONAL PARK, in the northwest corner of Montana

Founded: 1910

How Big: Glacier is 1.4 million acres big and includes over two hundred lakes.

Who Lives There: Mountain goats, bighorn sheep, black bear, grizzly bear, elk, white-tailed deer, mule deer, and moose make up the big mammals in the park. On the smaller side, beaver, river otter, marten, and pika can also be found. In the skies, look for bald eagle, golden eagle, ospreys, ptarmigan, Clark's Nutcracker, and the Harlequin duck.

What's to Do: Hike Glacier's 730 miles of trails to get a good understanding of what this outstanding park has to offer.

Take a drive. The Going-to-the-Sun Road is a fifty-mile breathtaking drive that runs the edge of the Continental Divide and the shores of the park's two largest lakes.

Explore over two hundred lakes of all sizes nestled within the park, keeping in mind that only a handful are accessible by car. Trout, salmon, northern pike, and burbot are among the fish available for the catching.

Cool Stuff: Fifty glaciers make this park very cool and likely played a key role in the naming of the park.

Lake McDonald does not serve any fast food but is the largest lake within the park at ten miles in length and a maximum depth of 472 feet. It was carved by a glacier estimated to be 2,200 feet thick.

Glacier National Park borders Waterton Lakes National Park in Canada; the combined parks are commonly referred to as the Waterton/Glacier International Peace Park, symbolizing the peaceful, friendly bond between the two countries.

The forty-ninth parallel divides the countries and acts as the border between the parks.

Junior Ranger Program: Yes

Park Neighbors: Yellowstone in southern Montana, Banff National Park just to the north in the Alberta province, and Yoho National Park and Kootenay National Park, located just inside the British Columbia border with Alberta

YOSEMITE NATIONAL PARK, in the east central part of California

Founded: 1890

How Big: This park comprises a very special 761,266 acres.

Who lives there: Mountain lions, marmot, badgers, bighorn sheep, black bear, mule deer, and coyotes are some of the prominent park residents.

What's to do: Eight hundred miles of hiking trails, rock climbing, and scenic drives to see giant sequoias are some of the key activities Yosemite has to offer.

You can also take a summer stagecoach ride at Wawona and visit the nature center at Happy Isles; it has a great play space for kids.

Cool Stuff: El Capitan, the most prominent and widely recognized landmark of Yosemite, is a year-round destination for rock climbers from around the world.

Yosemite is also home to the giant sequoia that can grow 160 to 279 feet tall. The sequoia known as "The Grizzly Giant" is the largest tree in the park, with a base ninety feet in circumference, thirty feet in diameter, and limbs in excess of one hundred feet. The Grizzly Giant is a very youthful 2,700 years old!

The Tunnel View is one of the most extensively photographed views of the park.

Junior Ranger Program: Yes

Park Neighbors: Kings Canyon National Park, Sequoia National Park, Death Valley National Park, and Point Reyes National Seashore are all within the state of California

GRAND CANYON NATIONAL PARK, located in the northwest corner of Arizona

Founded: 1919

How Big: At 1,218,376 acres, this mighty park encompasses America's biggest hole! As it stretches along the Colorado River, it is 277 miles long.

Who lives there: Mountain lion, mule deer, bighorn sheep, gray fox, bobcat, weasel, raccoon, and beaver are all native to the canyon.

What's to Do: Stand at the rim of the Grand Canyon and absorb the vast openness that lies in front of your family.

Take donkey rides along the narrow trails that skirt the canyon walls.

Hike, keeping in mind that grades can be steep for young children.

Go rafting down the Colorado River.

Cool Stuff: The Grand Canyon took three to six million years to form from the flowage of the Colorado River.

This river averages three hundred feet in width, one hundred feet in depth, and flows at an average speed of four miles per hour.

The depth of the Grand Canyon ranges between five thousand to six thousand vertical feet at its deepest point, which is approximately one vertical mile deep.

The Grand Canyon is considered one of the natural wonders of the world because of its unique natural features and its strata exposure, offering one of the most complete geological histories that can be seen anywhere in the world.

Junior Ranger Program: Yes

Park Neighbors: Hoover Dam near the Arizona/Nevada border, Bryce Canyon National Park, and Zion National Park are located just inside the Utah border to the north

STATE PARKS

Hundreds of state parks lie within close proximity to many of their larger national park kin. During your travel planning, state parks should also be considered as part of your family's road trip adventure. Many state parks offer great fishing, hiking, biking, and camping opportunities as well as other family-based outdoor recreational activities that vary by park and natural landscape.

The state parks can be a great added bonus to your family's road trip adventure by offering a variety of natural features and recreational opportunities that may not be available at the neighboring national parks.

Each and every state manages its park system independently. The best place to start your state park travel plan is to search that particular state's park system on-line. Coordinating a national/state park combo trip can be an awesome way to maximize your travel experience within your destination state.

PARK RANGER PET PEEVES

Park rangers in the U.S. and park wardens in Canada see tourists of all kinds. The vast majority of park visitors are a collective joy to have as park guests. However, a few consistent practices by some guests truly frustrate our park caretakers. While on your park adventure, please keep in mind the following tips, which will help preserve the park for future guests:

1. DO NOT FEED THE ANIMALS! It's not safe for you and it's typically a worse scenario for the animals.

2. Leave the park better than you found it. Pack any litter you create out of the park and please pick up any that is left from other careless visitors.

3. Do not mess with the cairn markers. These little piles of rocks are significant in marking trailheads and points of interest. Also, the long established markers have developed their own internal ecosystem that is immediately disrupted when the rocks are moved.

4. Stay on the trail and heed any warning signs. Park visitors are their own worst enemies at times, and typically, any harm that comes their way is their own doing.

5. Do not bring firewood to the parks. A number of invasive insects call firewood home. Your firewood could transport an invasive visitor that could have devastating effects on the ecology within the park.

6. Do not speed while driving through the parks. Speed limits are posted for the safety of tourists and animals alike.

CANADIAN NATIONAL PARKS SYSTEM

The Canadian National Park System showcases some of the wildest, scenic, and most remote stretches of land on earth today. Many of these parks are nothing short of unbelievable in their magnitude. However, from the perspective of a young family, some of the national parks are simply too remote or rugged to be considered a practical destination for a family road trip adventure. However, many great Canadian national parks are within a reasonable distance and can be reached by families on both sides of the border, including the following:

BANFF NATIONAL PARK, on the western edge of the Alberta province

Founded:	1885
How Big:	This famous park is made up of 2,564 square miles, or 6,641 square kilometers.
Who Lives There:	Grizzly and black bears, mule, white-tailed deer, elk, caribou, mountain goats, bighorn sheep, cougars, otters, badgers, mink, gray wolf, shrews, bats, pikas, and hares call Banff home.
What's to Do:	Hiking, fishing, and backpacking are popular family activities. Rock climbing appeals to adults as does scuba diving in Lake Minnewanka.
	The Johnston Canyon hike is only 1.7 miles (2.7 kilometers) one way and encompasses two breathtaking waterfalls. The lower falls are .7 miles (1.1 kilometers) into the trail and the upper falls are 1.7 miles down the trail. The trail skirts along the face of steep canyon walls with Johnston Creek rushing beneath your feet. CAUTION! Kids and adults need to stay on this trail and not venture into the creek. The currents are very powerful and accidents can quickly occur.
Cool Stuff:	Banff is Canada's very first national park and was founded when warm mineral springs were discovered deep inside a cave.
	Banff is one of the only parks that has animal crossing overpasses for the safe passage of wildlife across the road system within the park.
Park Neighbors:	Yoho National Park and Kootenay National Park just west across the British Columbia/Alberta border and Glacier National Park in British Columbia

PUKASKWA NATIONAL PARK, in central Ontario on the north shore of Lake Superior

Founded:	1978
How Big:	This park is 1,878 square kilometers, or 728 square miles.
Who Lives There:	White-tailed deer, black bear, moose, bald eagle, and the common loon live in Pukaskwa National Park, along with Canadian Geese (naturally).
What's to Do:	Kayak, Canoe, Hydro-bike the scenic, protected waters of Hattie Cove
	Fish the adjacent Pic River for a chance at numerous freshwater species
	Hike the breath taking shoreline, over lava bubbles to a sandy Horseshoe Beach
	Take a dip in the eternally chilly waters of the Great Lake Superior
	Take a full day hike that includes a trek across a 23m high suspension bridge, spanning over the Chigamiwinigum Falls
Cool Stuff:	This park is located on the north shore of Lake Superior, the biggest of the Great Lakes, and the largest body of fresh water in the world.
Park Neighbors:	Quetico Provincial Park to the west, along the southern Ontario and Minnesota state borders

WOOD BUFFALO NATIONAL PARK, located along the Alberta/Northwest Territories border

Founded:	1922
How Big:	In Latin, this park would be referred to as Parkus Maximus, coming in at 44,807 square kilometers, or 17,300 square miles big! This is by far Canada's largest national park...It's larger than the country of Switzerland big!
Who Lives There:	This park is home to over five thousand wood bison, the largest mammal native to North America, along with whooping cranes, moose, lynx, wolverines, peregrine falcons, eagles, owls, and the not-so-common red-sided garter snake.
What's to Do:	Walk the salt plains barefoot on powdery crystals and taste brine from an underground river.
	Get a front row seat to the Aurora Borealis light show (commonly known as the Northern Lights).
	Walk the scenic Karstland Loop Trail.
Cool Stuff:	This park is home to the largest beaver dam in the world. It's so big, it's visible from outer space!
	Wood Buffalo National Park is also home to the last remaining wild nesting site of the endangered whooping crane.
	Due to its location, Wood Buffalo National Park has seasons in which the sun shines twenty-four hours a day!

FUNDY NATIONAL PARK OF CANADA, in southern New Brunswick

Founded:	1948
How Big:	Fundy is made up of 206 square kilometers, or 79.5 square miles.
Who Lives There:	Moose, black bear, marten, fisher, and over 255 species of birds call Fundy home.
What's to Do:	Take a beach walk across the ocean floor during low tide on what is called the Intertidal zone.
	Bird watch the vast array of fowl that call Fundy home.
	Explore one hundred-plus kilometers of hiking trails along the coast and mountain range.
Cool Stuff:	Fundy is best known for having the highest high tides in the world.
	Fundy is home to the world's oldest known red spruce at 455 years and counting.
	You could stay in a yurt (and it won't hurt); it's just a very cool, round building.

ST. LAWRENCE ISLANDS NATIONAL PARK, in Ontario, in the Thousand Islands Region

Founded:	1904
How Big:	The smallest park in the system, St. Lawrence Islands National Park contains 24.4 square kilometers, or 9.4 square miles, encompassing twenty-one islands.
Who Lives There:	White-tailed deer, fox, porcupine, and coyotes live here.
What's to Do:	Kayaking, canoeing, island camping, boating, sailing, swimming, and geocaching are all popular.
Cool Stuff:	This was the first Canadian park founded east of the Rockies. It is home to a preserved hull of a British gunboat from the War of 1812 and is close to urban areas, so it's readily accessible to many visitors.
Park Neighbors:	Algonquin Provincial Park to the north, within the Ontario Province

GULF ISLANDS NATIONAL PARK, in southwest British Columbia

Founded:	2003
How Big:	This park is thirty-six square kilometers, or 13.9 square miles, and encompasses fifteen islands.
Who Lives There:	Orcas, porpoises, otters, sea lions, and seals all inhabit Gulf Islands.
What's to Do:	Shoreline hiking, exploring shoreline rock formations, sailing, sea kayaking, power boating, and swimming are all popular activities.
Cool Stuff:	Gulf Islands is what a water park was truly meant to be!
Park Neighbors:	Strathcona Provincial Park, Garibaldi Provincial Park, and Golden Ears Provincial Park, all located within southwest British Columbia

POINT PELEE NATIONAL PARK, in the southeastern corner of Ontario

Founded: 1918

How Big: This park is relatively small at just fifteen square kilometers, or 5.8 square miles.

Who Lives There: Weasels, mink, skunks, coyotes, raccoons, grey squirrels, and lots of migrating birds live at Point Pelee.

What's to Do: Limited hiking, kayaking, swimming, and bird watching are big here.

Cool Stuff: Point Pelee is renowned as the best location in North America to see the spring migration of northbound songbirds.

It is also the temporary autumn home to thousands of Monarch butterflies as they begin their annual migration to Mexico.

Park Neighbors: Fort Malden National Historic Site, just to the east, and Georgian Bay Islands National Park, located further north within the Ontario Province

BRUCE PENINSULA NATIONAL PARK and **FATHOM FIVE NATIONAL MARINE PARK**, located in southeastern Ontario along the western Georgian Bay shore, are next-door neighbors and share a common visitor centre located in Fathom Five National Marine Park.

Founded: 1987

How Big: Bruce National Park is 150 square kilometers, or 58 square miles; Fanthom National Park is 112 square kilometers, or 43.2 square miles.

Who Lives There: White-tailed deer, snowshoe hare, fox, marten, and black bear live here.

What's to Do: Hike some of the fifty-five kilometers of trails within the park, some of which make up the Niagara Escarpment, Canada's oldest and longest trail system.

Explore the magnificent rocky shoreline along crystal clear, beautiful blue waters.

Visit a freshwater grotto with a hidden pool and underwater cave entrance; the water is so cold, it will give your freezer a run for its money!

Visit underwater shipwrecks, perfectly preserved by the cool, clear waters of Georgian Bay, by glass bottom tour boat, SCUBA diving, or snorkeling adventure.

Tour Flower Pot Island and its unique stone columns.

Cool Stuff: Cedar trees as old as 511 to 850 years old take root within this park.

The Bruce Peninsula National Park contains the largest contiguous forest in southern Ontario.

An awesome visitor centre located in the Fathom Five National Marine Park and shared by both parks features a natural museum and wildlife display.

Fathom Five is Canada's first national marine conservation area.

Park Neighbors: Georgian Bay Islands National Park, just across Georgian Bay on the east shoreline

PRINCE ALBERT NATIONAL PARK OF CANADA, in Central Saskatchewan

Founded:	1927
How Big:	This park is 3,875 square kilometers, or about 1,500 square miles.
Who Lives There:	Wolves, fox, bald eagles, beaver, stag elk, bison, and over 240 bird species call Prince Albert home.
What's to Do:	Cycling, canoeing, bird watching, and limited hiking are all popular.
	You can also play the "Match the Poop" game at the visitor center and hike the Waska river trail.
Cool Stuff:	Prince Albert is home to the second largest breeding colony of white pelicans in the world as well as home to author, woodsman, and conservationist Grey Owl, who died in 1938.
Park Neighbors:	Meadow Lake Provincial Park, Candle Lake, and La Ronge Provincial Park

RIDING MOUNTAIN NATIONAL PARK OF CANADA, in western Manitoba

Founded:	1930
How Big:	This park is three thousand square kilometers, or 1,158 square miles.
Who Lives There:	Wolves, moose, black bear, captive bison, and elk live in this park.
What's to Do:	Horseback riding is big here, with over four hundred kilometers of trails split between horse trails and regular hiking trails.
Cool Stuff:	This national park housed the Whitewater P.O.W. camp for German prisoners of war during World War II. From 1943 to 1945, German prisoners logged the area for heating wood. Due to the remoteness of the park, no fences were needed to contain them!
Park Neighbors:	Atikaki Provincial Park, Nopiming Provincial Park, and Whiteshell Provincial Park are each located along the eastern border of the Manitoba province, while Hecla-Grindstone Provincial Park is also located in southeast Manitoba

GEORGIAN BAY ISLANDS NATIONAL PARK,

located in southeast Ontario along the eastern Georgian Bay shore

Founded:	1929
How Big:	Eastern Canada's third national park, Georgian Bay Islands contains twelve square kilometers, or 4.6 square miles, encompassing fifty-nine islands.
Who Lives There:	A variety of reptiles and amphibians including the massasauga rattlesnake, frogs, and turtles live here.
What's to Do:	Boating, sailing, open water kayaking, swimming, limited hiking, and great bird watching are all available here.
Cool Stuff:	Beausoleil Island is the largest island in the park, providing the perfect escape from the city. It is commonly referred to as "cottage country."

Wasaga Beach is the longest freshwater beach in the world.

Park Neighbors: Bruce Peninsula National Park of Canada just across Georgian Bay and Algonquin Provincial Park to the northeast, towards the Ontario/Quebec border

PROVINCIAL PARKS

There are numerous breathtaking provincial parks within each of the Canadian provinces. The enormity and ruggedness of some of these provincial parks leaves you hard pressed to discern them from their national park kin. Province-specific annual park passes are available that allow entry into all provincial parks within that province. Provincial parks are classified in four ways; each offers different opportunities for family recreation, wilderness experiences, natural environment viewing, or historical education.

Wilderness parks are dedicated to the preservation of expansive natural areas that have been untouched by modern development.

Natural environment parks also preserve large areas of land in a natural state yet allow recreational activities in smaller areas of the park.

Recreation parks, while still protecting the land within their boundaries, offer a broad range of recreational activities.

Historic parks and historic sites represent significant areas that played a key historic role within that province.

So significant are many of Canada's provincial parks that they alone can be awesome destinations on your family road trip adventures.

★ CROSS BORDER TRAVEL 🍁

If you are venturing across the United States/Canada border, in either direction, make sure you have all the proper paperwork with you for each person traveling in your vehicle. Verify ahead of time exactly what documents are needed for both countries and keep them readily accessible as you approach the border. Also be aware of what can AND CANNOT be legally transported across the border. Being properly prepared and fully legal will save you time and help you avoid lengthy detainment as you traverse the border.

Random Thoughts About the Outdoors

Spotting tourists who have spotted animals is often times easier than spotting the animals themselves!

Wildlife, it's in the name. It's wild and full of life. Immerse yourself in it!

The early eyes get the surprise!

Ranger, Ranger, where's the danger?

The Perfect Smore — not the food, the experience. It's so great, you'll want S'more. Not just coincidence as it typically caps a great day of adventure in one or more of our awesome parks

People Game — How close can we get to that animal?

Animal Game — How dumb do they come?

Campfires to wildfires are but one spark away. If it's dry and windy, no fires, eat your marshmallow cold.

Education: You can learn a lot from nature, though mostly about yourself!

If you give a moose a fright, you will end up in his sight!

Nature of the Parks
You can see it. You can hear it. You can definitely smell it. You can touch it and even taste it. But you need to leave it be - physically, capturing only it's memories!

S-L-O-W D-O-W-N

Don't speed past the moose, or the elk, or the eagle...or most importantly...don't speed past the time with your family

Trail Limits: The extent of your kid's is the extent of your hike!

And finally...
A family that experiences nature together, stays together and a family that stays together, well, is really just that indeed, a family that stays together!

AWESOME ANIMALS

OF THE
NATIONAL PARKS

BALD EAGLE

Fun Fax:

- Bald Eagles have amazing eyesight, 8 times more powerful than that of people

- Bald Eagles can fly up to altitudes of 10,000' (without having to wait in long security lines to do so)

- Bald Eagles are not bald at all, but have white feathers on both their head and tail

- Bald Eagles are very loyal in that they mate for life

- Bald Eagle nests are called an Aeries which they may use for many years (this saves the eagle a lot on moving and remodeling expenses)

- Bald Eagle females are normally bigger than the male (so the male never speaks out of turn)

Name: Comes from the English word 'balde' which means white

It is the national symbol for the United States of America

Life Span: Average between 15 to 20 years in the wild

Size: Average weight is between 10 and 14 lbs, with a wing span between 72" to 90"

Food: Fish is the primary diet, with small mammals and carrion also on the eagle menu

Let's make tracks!

53

BEAVER

Name: The national symbol of Canada

Life Span: Can live up to 24 years in the wild

Size: Can weigh up to 60 lbs (that is one big, tree cutting machine)

Food: Herbivores, eating bark, leaves, twigs, roots and aquatic plants or water lily tubers

Fun Fax:
- Beaver babies are called 'kits'
- Beaver homes are called 'lodges' (but do not have fireplaces)
- Beavers can stay underwater for up to 15 minutes, and swim up to 5 mph
- Beavers will smack their tail on the water when startled
- Beavers are the second largest rodent in the world
- Beavers have transparent eyelids that function like underwater goggles
- Beavers are second only to humans, in their ability to change their environment (and they can build their dams without having to pull any permits)
- A group of beavers is called a colony

Let's make tracks!

54

BLACK BEAR

Fun Fax:

- Black Bears have very poor eyesight, but an amazing sense of smell

- Black Bears are shy and typically avoid human contact once they get their scent

- Black Bear moms are very protective of their young

- Black Bear moms birth between 1 and 3 cubs during their winter hibernation (since all the other bears are sleeping too, they do not have baby cub showers)

- Black Bears are good tree climbers (but are not good to share a tree house with)

Name: Clearly named for it's color, but the same species can be blonde or cinnamon (scientists do not yet know if a blonde black bear really has more fun)

Boys are Boars (but it doesn't mean they are boring to hang with)

Girls are Sows

Life Span: Average up to 20 years

Size: Adult black bears can weigh between 200 and 600 pounds

Food: Omnivores, (like teenagers, they eat everything and lots of it) berries, insects, nuts, grasses, meat

Let's make tracks!

GRIZZLY BEAR

Name: Comes from their 'grizzled' appearance caused by long, white-tipped hair on their neck and shoulders (the exact opposite personality of your cuddly teddy bear)

Boys are Boars

Girls are Sows

Life Span: Average life span is 15 to 20 years, but have reached 25 years in the wild

Size: Sows average 350 to 800 lbs, while Boars average between 500 and 1,000 lbs (now that's a BIG bear!)

Food: Omnivores, from mice to moose and berries to fish, often times eating 'carrion' (which is leftovers to wildlife)

Fun Fax:

- Grizzly moms give birth every third year to one to three cubs

- Grizzly bears can be extremely dangerous and tend to click their teeth just before attack

- Grizzly bears are the second largest member of the bear family (Neither Yogi or Baloo are members of the grizzly bear family)

- Grizzly bears are excellent fishermen (but will never tell what they use for bait or speak of their hot spot)

Let's make tracks!

56

COYOTE

Fun Fax:

- Coyotes are fast runners, reaching speeds of 40 mph

- Coyotes mate for life (which saves on dating expenses)

- Coyote groups are referred to as packs

- Coyotes have excellent vision and a super duper sense of smell

- Coyotes are very resourceful scavengers and hunters allowing them to live just about anywhere

- Coyotes hunt small prey on their own, but will work as a team to hunt larger prey, such as deer

- 3 to 12 pups are born in a litter

Name: Comes from the Mexican Spanish language, and whose name means 'barking dog'

Life Span: Average life span is 5 to 10 years

Size: Adults can weigh between 20 and 50 lbs

Food: Omnivores, eating everything from rabbits to rodents, to frogs and fish, mice and deer, But will eat insects, fruits and berries as well.

Let's make tracks!

GREY WOLF

Name: Despite its name, can vary greatly in color

Life Span: Average life span is 6 to 8 years, but have made it to 13 years in the wild

Size: Average between 60 and 150 lbs

Food: Carnivores, eating deer, elk, moose, caribou, beaver and other small mammals

Fun Fax:

- Grey wolves have grey, black or light brown fur on the heads and body, often times with yellowish or white fur on their legs and belly

- Grey wolves, despite their name, could be all white or all black too

- Grey wolves live in packs of 2 to 12 animals

- Grey wolves are born blind but gain their sight within 9 to 12 days

- Grey wolves can consume up to 20 pounds of meat in a single sitting (again, a very similar eating pattern as that of a human teenager)

- Grey wolves can hear another wolf howling from 3 to 4 miles away (so you can just imagine how loud wolf family gatherings can be)

Let's make tracks!

58

BISON

Fun Fax:

- Bison are the heaviest land mammal in North America
- Bison are fast for their size, running up to 40 mph
- Bison have curved shaped horns that can grow up to 2' in length
- Bison Bulls have wider heads than Bison Cows
- Bison have a large hump of muscle between their shoulders to support their big heads (but are not considered to be arrogant)
- Bison have poor vision (glasses don't fit their large heads), but have great sniffers and ears
- Bison raise their tail straight up when they are mad and ready to attack!

Name: Comes from a Greek word meaning 'ox-like' animal

Boys are Bulls

Girls are Cows

Life Span: Can live up to 15 to 20 years in the wild

Size: Cows can weigh between 800 and 1,000 lbs, up to 5' at the shoulder

Bulls can weigh between 1,000 and 2,000 lbs, up to 6' at the shoulder

Food: Herbivores, eating plains grasses, twigs and shrubs

Let's make tracks!

CARIBOU

Name: Comes from a native American word that means 'snow scraper' and are the only member of the deer family in which both the male and female have antlers

Boys are Bulls or Bucks

Girls are Cows

Life Span: Can live up to 15 years in the wild

Size: Weight can vary between 250 and 700 lbs

Food: Herbivore, eating up to 12 lbs of lichens, plants and grasses daily

Fun Fax:

- Caribou can run up to 50 mph

- Caribou have a loose area of skin on their throat covered in white hair called a 'dewlap'

- Caribou have an outer layer of fur made up of straight hollow hairs that insulate it from the cold

- Caribou hooves are adaptive acting like snow shoes for deep snow and paddles for water (which keeps their shoe costs down dramatically)

- Caribou give off a scent when sensing danger to alert other caribou

- Caribou can sleep in water

Let's make tracks!

60

MOOSE

Size: Height can reach 5' to 6.5' at the shoulder

Bulls can weigh between 800 and 1,600 lbs (making them the largest member of the deer family)

Cows can weigh between 600 and 800 lbs (A cow moose never asks a bull moose if their fur makes them look fat)

Food: Herbivores (the animal version of a vegetarian), eating grasses, shrubs and twigs

Fun Fax:

- Moose antlers can grow over 6' wide in just 4 months time (bulls only)

- Moose do not have upper teeth (so a 50% less chance of getting cavities)

- Moose have poor eyesight (but look silly with glasses)

- Moose have great sniffers and ears

- Moose can run up to 35 mph, are strong swimmers and can stay under water for up to 30 seconds

- Moose have long faces (but are not depressed)

- Moose have a skin flap that hangs beneath their throat called a 'bell' (do not try to ring it)

- Moose have 1 to 2 calves in the spring, averaging 30 lbs. (yes, that means very big diapers)

Name: Comes from the Alongquin Indian word meaning 'twig eater'

Boys are Bulls

Girls are Cows (but we mean that in a nice way)

Life Span: 15 to 20 years (moose love surprise birthday parties)

Let's make tracks!

ELK

Name: Comes from the Shawnee Indian name Wapiti, meaning 'white rump'
(Also applicable to human sun bathers)

Boys are Bulls

Girls are Cows

Life Span: 8 to 12 years
(slightly less for those with high stress jobs, and junk food diets)

Size: Heights can reach 4' to 5' at the shoulder

Bulls can reach 700 lbs

Cows top out around 500 lbs (possibly from picking up after the bull)

Food: Herbivores (and willing to eat their plants without Ranch dressing)

Fun Fax:

- Cows birth one calf in early summer, averaging 35 lbs (so even bigger diapers)

- Bull elk make a loud noise during mating season called 'bugling' (which is the elk version of texting their girlfriends)

- Elk, like all members of the deer family, have a great sense of smell

- Elk antlers also grow in just 4 short months, falling off in early winter (bulls only)

- Bull Elk roll in large mud pits called 'wallows' during the mating season (but they do not track this into the house)

Let's make tracks!

MULE DEER

Size: Mule deer can weigh between 125 and 300 lbs

Food: Herbivores, eating prairie grasses and other plants

Fun Fax:

- Mule deer young are called fawns, and birth 1 to 2 each spring
- Mule deer have very big ears and are excellent listeners (but very difficult to sit one down for a good conversation)
- Mule deer have a distinctive bounding leap called 'stouting', reaching 45 mph
- Mule deer bucks grow antlers with 2 main beams to each antler (different from their white-tailed cousins who only have one main beam to each antler)
- Mule deer, like other members of the deer family are 'crepuscular' in nature (which means they are most active in the lowlight (dawn and dusk) periods of the day)

Name: Its long, mule-like ears provide it's name (but don't try to ride one or put a pack on it)

Boys are Bucks (but it doesn't mean they have a lot of money)

Girls are Does (and the girls name has nothing to do with baking)

Life Span: 9 to 11 years in the wild

Mule Deer Antlers

Let's make tracks!

63

WHITE TAIL DEER

Name: Comes from the underside of its tail which is raised when it is startled or alarmed (or jittery about the stock market)

Boys are Bulls

Girls are Cows

Life Span: Up to 20 years in the wild, up to 23 years in captivity (zoo life)

Size: Adults can reach between 100 and 300 pounds

Food: Herbivore, grasses, crops, apples, corn, leaves (and just about anything planted outside your house)

Fun Fax:

- Whitetails are awesome jumpers clearing fences 10' high and covering up to 30' In a single bound

- Whitetails have great eyesight, hearing and sense of smell

- Whitetail birth 1 to 3 fawns each spring, whose light brown coat is covered with a couple hundred white spots

- Whitetail fawns have no odor at birth so predators cannot find them (and it makes for a really fresh smelling nursery

White Tail Deer Antlers

Let's make tracks!

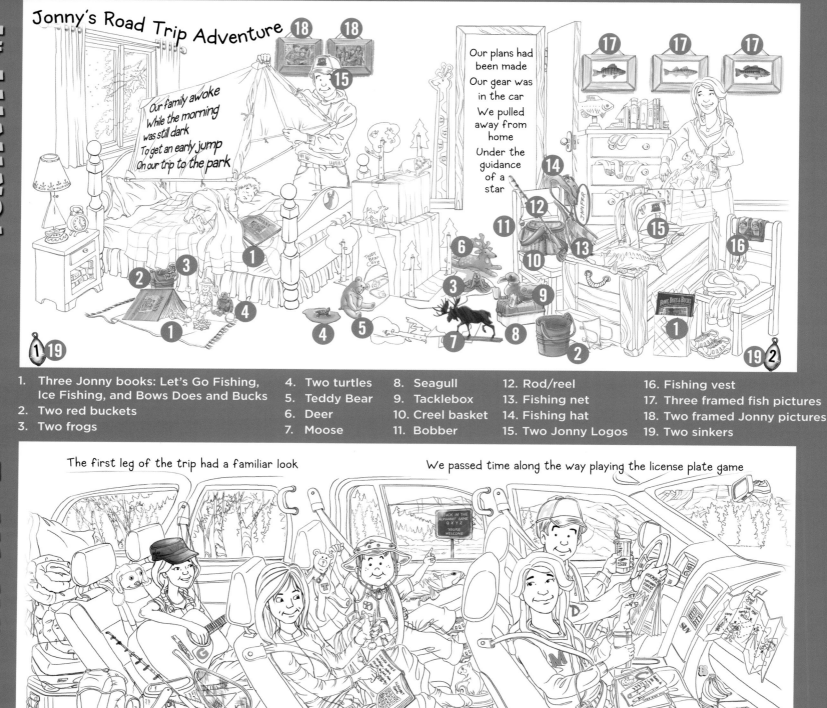

Jonny's Road Trip Adventure

Our family awoke
While the morning
was still dark
To get an early jump
On our trip to the park

Our plans had
been made
Our gear was
in the car
We pulled
away from
home
Under the
guidance
of a
star

1. Three Jonny books: Let's Go Fishing, Ice Fishing, and Bows Does and Bucks
2. Two red buckets
3. Two frogs
4. Two turtles
5. Teddy Bear
6. Deer
7. Moose
8. Seagull
9. Tacklebox
10. Creel basket
11. Bobber
12. Rod/reel
13. Fishing net
14. Fishing hat
15. Two Jonny Logos
16. Fishing vest
17. Three framed fish pictures
18. Two framed Jonny pictures
19. Two sinkers

The first leg of the trip had a familiar look

We passed time along the way playing the license plate game

So my sisters and I settled in with a book

Eyeing each car that we saw to see from where it came

65

Find the 26 letters of the alphabet.

When we awoke we were far from the city

The mountains were so **HUGE** They made us all feel itty-bitty

1. Fundy
2. Grand Canyon
3. Pukaskwas
4. Glacier
5. Banff
6. Yellowstone
7. Redwood
8. Everglades
9. Acadia
10. Jasper

When hunger joined the family
We found a local diner
To get a taste of an area
You can't find food
that's any finer

1. Six cups
2. Two food baskets
3. Six stools
4. Eight People
5. Four salt shakers
6. Four sugar jars
7. Four napkin holders
8. Four ketchup bottles
9. Four mustard bottles
10. Six Pies

We continued down the road, Our tummies' wants had been met But soon I had to ask...

"Mom and Dad, are we there yet?"

Find numbers from 1 to 20.

We pulled into the park
With oh so much to see
But before we did a thing

The whole family had to wee

1. Seven spelling errors
2. Fall leaves on tree
3. Dad entering women's restroom
4. "300 yards to right" arrow points left
5. Jonny missing shoe
6. One tire is square
7. Mismatched socks
8. Different color doors
9. Fire danger says "wet"
10. Snow on pine tree

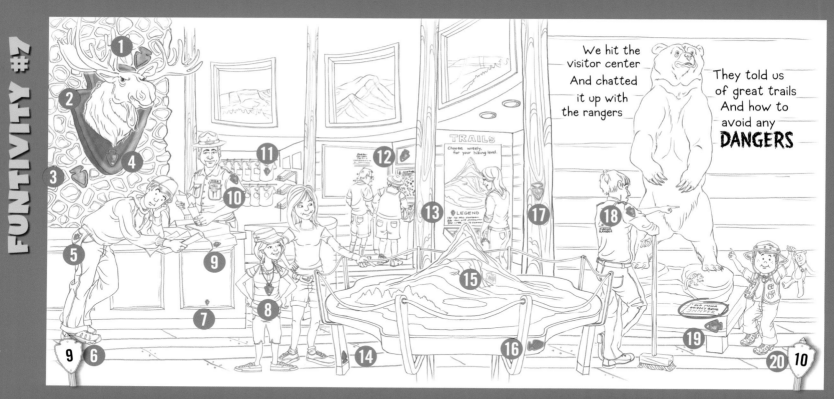

Find 20 National Park arrow symbols

1. Three backpacks
2. Cooler
3. Teddy Bear
4. Lantern
5. Flyswatter
6. Stove in case
7. Propane kit
8. Two sleeping bags
9. Four suitcases
10. Flashlight
11. Fishing gear
12. Red bucket

Find 16 Adventures With Jonny logos

The trailhead had begun
Winding through a twisty pine alley
That led us to a very high bluff
Overlooking a sun-filled valley

Elk and deer
were everywhere
Doing their
daytime grazing
This view was to our family
Nothing short of amazing

Count the number of deer in each herd:
1. Twelve elk   2. Five mule deer   3. Eleven Bison   4. Five caribou   5. Two moose   6. Eight whitetail deer

We continued on our hike
To a great waterfall
My teenage sister said
"You won't see that
at any mall"

Mom whipped out her camera
And said, "Picture time, please"
Pushed us into a group
And then we all said

"CHEESE!"

We stopped for a break
By a babbling little creek
That's when we saw a snake
And my sister did the

FREAK

Find eight animal tracks: 1. Wolf   2. Beaver   3. Deer   4. Coyote   5. Grizzly Bear   6. Moose   7. Elk   8. Black Bear

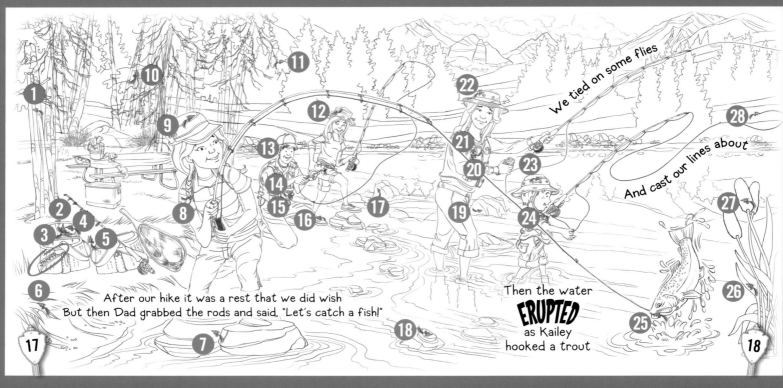

After our hike it was a rest that we did wish
But then Dad grabbed the rods and said, "Let's catch a fish!"

We tied on some flies

And cast our lines about

Then the water
ERUPTED
as Kailey
hooked a trout

Find 28 fishing flies

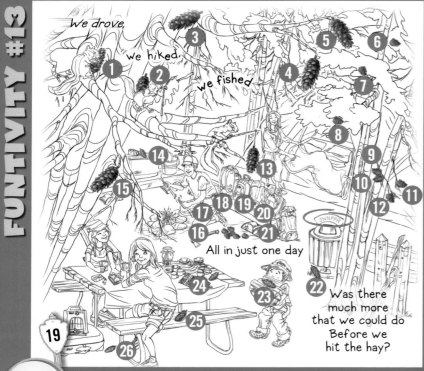

We drove,

we hiked,

we fished

All in just one day

Was there
much more
that we could do
Before we
hit the hay?

Find 26 pine cones

Well a sunset was to be
The next thing that we did see
The horizon blazed in orange
With my family next to me

The day
drew to a close
As we settled in our site
Where we built a warm bonfire
Under a starry, starry night

Find 7 sets of 7 fireflies and 5 sets of 7 firefly glows

69

Find 29 Chipmunks

Find the word "Thrive" 14 times

THE AUTHOR

Michael A. DiLorenzo (who really prefers Mike) is a married father of three residing in the outdoor-rich environs of the great state of Michigan. Mike created the Adventures with Jonny series to entertain and educate children about the great outdoors and the adventures that eagerly await them.

"If you give a child the gift of the outdoors, you give them a gift for life" are words that Mike lives by and came up with while on his own, in the middle of nowhere, doing what he loves to do most, simply being outdoors.

Look for all the Adventures with Jonny titles and the newest outdoor Jonny Gear on the Adventures with Jonny website at www.adventureswithjonny.com.

THE ILLUSTRATOR

It's entirely the illustrators' fault, actually. When illustrating the first Jonny book, Jenniffer included her signature in a variety of hidden ways on the illustrations. Her intension was to NOT be overt in the signing locations, but she accidentally created a fun task for readers – find her abbreviated name … JNNFFR. Kids loved to locate the artist name so she continued to hide it in books 2 and 3.

When book 4 came along, the author had an epiphany! As it was about a road trip, he wanted to add an activity component to keep little ones occupied on the journey. It was determined that each illustration would include a different 'funtivity'. This doubled the creative work. It also doubled the fun!

As principal artist of Jnnffr Productions (www.jnnffr.com), she hopes you have as much fun finding the hidden items, as she did drawing them. She did get a little carried away at times; you could say she went a bit squirrely, or is that chipmunky?